The Serpent's Cave

Ann Turnbull

Illustrated by Alan Marks

Hodder
Children's
Books

a division of Hodder Headline Limited

Text copyright © 2000 by Ann Turnbull
Illustrations copyright © 2000 by Alan Marks

First published in Great Britain in 2000
by Hodder Children's Books

ISBN 0340 77942 X

Printed and bound in Great Britain by
The Guernsey Press Company Ltd,
Guernsey, Channel Islands

Hodder Children's Books
A Division of Hodder Headline Limited
338 Euston Road
London NW1 3BH

Contents

To David and Julie

Chapter One

The New Queen

There was once a king who had two children: a boy named Hugh, and a girl named Maisie. They lived in a grey stone castle on a high grey cliff above the sea.

The queen had died long ago, and the king was often away from the castle, travelling about his kingdom, which stretched for many miles of seashore and moor and forest. Hugh and Maisie, left in the care of their nurse and the servants, were allowed to do much as they pleased.

The castle was old and run-down, but the children didn't care about that. In winter they ran and played hide-and-seek in the great draughty rooms and stone corridors, while outside the sea boomed and broke in spray on the rocks. When night came they sat with the dogs by a red fire in the hall and listened to a minstrel tell stories of ghosts and witches.

In summer they lived outside. They climbed the cliffs and raced on the beaches; they learnt to sail and swim. Out at sea, off the coast where the castle stood, was a rock called the Black Rock where sea birds nested and filled the air with their clamour. Beneath the rock was a deep cave. Here, Hugh and Maisie made a secret place for themselves.

The New Queen

Sometimes seals came to the cave, and the children played with them, diving and twisting in the water. They listened to the birds who nested on the rock above, listening so hard that they almost understood their language. One day Hugh rescued a fledgling gull that had fallen out of its nest. He gave it a name, Keir, that sounded like its cry. Before long it would fly to him whenever he called it.

The children were happy, but one spring a great change came into their lives. Their father returned from his travels with a new bride – a woman so beautiful that the air around her glimmered as she moved, and everyone who saw her said she must be of the fairy race. Her name was Inga.

The king summoned his children. "Inga will be a mother to you," he said.

Hugh, the eldest, could scarcely remember his true mother, and was not sure he needed one now. But he was glad to see his father happy. He bowed and said, "Good evening, Mother. You are welcome." And Maisie echoed his words.

Inga turned her blue gaze on Hugh and Maisie. She smiled, but her eyes were cold.

She hates us, thought Hugh. Maisie's hand crept into his, and he held it tightly.

The new queen blew through the cold grey castle like a bright breeze. She drove out the dogs, dismissed the lazy servants, and cast aside the faded but familiar rugs and hangings. In their place came shimmering cloths with serpentine patterns, brocade tapestries, velvet and silk, soft rugs underfoot, scented candles, spiced wine.

The king was enchanted. He loved Inga, and it seemed she loved him. She had brought with her a little harp made of bone, and on it she would play and sing – strange melodies that coiled around the heart like snakes. Hugh felt that if he listened too long he would be lost, and he saw how his father nodded and smiled, and how his eyes grew vacant as Inga sang.

Hugh and Maisie were no longer at ease in the castle. As summer came they stayed outside till dark. They climbed the cliffs, swam in the sea, talked to the gulls and choughs; and when it rained they sheltered in their cave under the Black Rock.

"I am afraid of Inga," said Maisie.

And Hugh said, "She has our father in her power. We must stay together, us two."

But it was not to be.

Chapter Two

Hugh's Journey

One evening, when the family sat by the fire, Inga put down her harp and said, "My lord, Hugh will soon be a man. Since he is your heir, he should learn the duties of a prince. Let me send him on a visit to my brother, the King of Silver Lake."

Hugh felt alarm. He shook his head – and Maisie ran to their father and fell on her knees and begged, "Don't send Hugh away!"

The king stroked Maisie's hair. "There is time enough, surely?" he asked his wife.

Inga smiled. "As you wish, my lord." She took up the bone harp and idly, it seemed, plucked sweet notes; her eyes never left the king's face. Hugh felt her power and knew his father was under an enchantment.

Nothing more was said that day, but next morning the king, with Inga beside him, told the children that he had agreed to their stepmother's plan.

Hugh mistrusted Inga more than ever. She wants to separate us, he thought. He turned to the queen: "Let Maisie come too. She should learn to be a princess."

But Inga smiled, and coiled her fingers in Maisie's brown hair. She said, "Maisie is still a child. And everything she needs to know she can learn from me."

The children swam out to their sea cave together for the last time.

The gulls flew around, and Hugh thought he heard them warning against Inga in their harsh voices. Keir perched on his shoulder.

"If the queen should threaten you while I am away," said Hugh, "send this bird to find me, and I will come at once. I won't let her harm you."

The next day Hugh set off on horseback with Inga's servant, a man named Randal, who was to deliver him to the King of Silver Lake.

Randal seemed friendly. He told Hugh of the delights of the King of Silver Lake's court: the hunting, the feasts, the music and dancing.

"And is it far?" asked Hugh.

"It's not so far," said Randal.

They stopped that night, and made camp, and ate and drank, and Hugh thought Randal looked downcast – but perhaps he was only tired from the long day's riding.

The next day, and the next, they journeyed on across moorland and through marsh and forest, and again Hugh asked, "Is it far?" and Randal said, "It's not so far." But again Hugh thought his companion looked sad.

On the seventh day they stopped as dusk fell in a great dark forest that seemed to have no end. The trees crowded in around them, and there was no path that Hugh could see. How did Randal know the way, he wondered? He began to feel uneasy.

"Where are you taking me?" he demanded.

At that, Randal turned to him. And to Hugh's alarm the man began to cry; he hid his face in his hands and sobbed. "We are here," he said at last. "At our journey's end."

Hugh looked around, at the forest and the deepening twilight. At last he understood – and turned cold with fear.

"There is no King of Silver Lake," said Randal. "The queen has no brother. She gave me gold and ordered me to take you to a deserted place, and kill you."

Hugh backed away in horror.

"Don't be afraid," said Randal. He reached out and put a hand on Hugh's shoulder. "I won't harm you. Every night, when we stopped, I told myself I would do the deed, but I couldn't and so we travelled on another day. But I must go back. I'll take your horse and tell the queen you are dead, and you must never be seen at the castle again."

"But my sister!" cried Hugh. He thought with anguish of Maisie. They had promised each other they would not be parted.

"Your sister is safe enough," said Randal. "It was you the queen feared: she knew that you saw through her enchantments and would grow up to challenge her."

But Maisie will fight her too, thought Hugh, and then *she'*ll be in danger. He clung to Randal. "Take me home! Please!"

"I dare not. The queen is a powerful fairy, and vengeful. She will come seeking us if I don't return. But I won't leave you here. We will find a safe place to sleep tonight."

Randal paced about, searching for a path. The dusk deepened; it was hard to tell tree from shadow, and the darkness under the branches was full of rustlings and scuttlings. Then Hugh heard a different sound: a short bark. He turned and saw a fox watching him. It sprang away, then stopped, and looked back at him, as if inviting him to follow, before trotting off again. And as Hugh's gaze followed its movement through the undergrowth he saw a path and, beyond it, a lighter area that could only be a clearing.

"This way!" he said.

They mounted their horses and rode on.

As they approached the clearing they saw that a woodcutter had been at work. There were stacked logs, and the path was pale with sawdust. And a little way off, amongst the trees, the light of a candle shone in a cottage window.

*

Thomas, the woodcutter, was an old man who lived alone near the edge of the forest. He agreed to give the travellers a bed for the night, but said he had little food to offer them.

Gratefully, they went inside. The three of them shared what they had, and somehow there was enough. Hugh thought the woodcutter's eyes were kind; he trusted him at once.

But he was tired. Thomas made him up a bed of straw in a corner of the room, and Hugh lay there half awake, aware of the two men talking. Once he heard the chink of coins.

In the morning, when Hugh woke, Randal was already dressed. He knelt to talk to the boy. "I am leaving you in the care of Thomas. He knows who you are. He is a good man and says he will treat you like his own child. I must go now, back to the queen. And you must stay here, where you are safe."

Hugh nodded, and they hugged each other. When Randal stood up to go, Hugh tried to look brave, as a king's son should. "Take care of my sister," he said.

"I will."

And with that promise Randal was gone.

Chapter Three

Maisie in Danger

Maisie was lonely without Hugh. Randal returned, and told her that her brother was safe with the King of Silver Lake.

"When will he come home?" asked Maisie.

Randal could not bear to tell her the truth. "A few months, perhaps," he said.

"Months!" cried Maisie. She wanted to be with Hugh more than anything.

And when the summer months were gone, and winter had come, and still she asked, "When?", Randal said, "No one travels in winter, lady. You must wait till spring." By spring, he hoped, the child would have stopped pining.

Maisie asked her
father about Hugh,
but he could not tell
her anything; he was
lost to her, beguiled
by Inga's spells. The
queen tried to draw
Maisie, too, into her
power. She gave the
girl gowns, and jewels
for her hair, but
Maisie would not wear
them; she roamed the
castle in her ragged
gown and bare feet,
longing for spring.

Even in winter Maisie escaped from the castle
whenever she could. And when spring came she
began once more to swim out to her cave under
the Black Rock. There she would sit amongst
the patterns of shifting light on the cave walls.
She would watch the seals with their newborn
pups and listen to the thousand voices of the

birds that nested above. Hugh's tame gull Keir came to her and perched on her shoulder.

Maisie stroked his feathers. "You are still our friend," she said.

Spring passed, and Hugh did not come home. Maisie overcame her fear of the queen, and demanded of her, "Where is my brother? What have you done to him?"

Inga laughed a little mocking laugh and said, "Dear child, he is enjoying all the pleasures of my brother's court. Did you think he would miss the foolish games he played with you? I am sure he has quite forgotten you."

Then Maisie swam out to the Black Rock and crept into her cave and cried.

She couldn't bear the thought that Hugh might forget her. He never would. And yet . . . he was so long away. Had Inga put him under some enchantment?

Maisie began to despair. I wish I could become a sea creature and stay here for ever, she thought.

*

Summer came and went, and another summer came. Maisie grew tall, and the ragged gown no longer fitted her, but she would not wear Inga's shimmering fabrics and jewels. Instead she stitched her own dresses out of plain brown stuff and wore her hair long over her shoulders. She was brown and strong and swam like a seal, and when she turned and twisted in the water she almost became the sea creature she had wished to be.

Inga mocked her. "You are as wet as a seal — and you smell like one too."

But one evening – a rare warm evening, when the stones of the castle held the sun's heat – the king and queen and Maisie sat at table beneath a high open window. Some servants were passing on the path below, chatting, unaware of the way their voices carried, and the words of one of them floated, clear as water, into the room:

"But do you see the Lady Maisie – how she's grown so tall, with her bonny brown hair and her dark eyes? It won't be long now before she outshines the queen."

There was silence in the hall.

The three of them stopped eating; even the serving maid stood still, with a dish in her hands. And everyone looked at Maisie.

Maisie felt her face redden. She was shocked and frightened. She had never thought of herself as bonny – never sought to rival the queen.

The king laughed and said, "What nonsense these people talk! Maisie is just a pretty child." And he signalled to the maid to close the window.

But Maisie felt the queen's gaze upon her, and knew that what the servant said was true, and that Inga's scorn had changed in an instant to hatred.

She knew, too, that she was now in danger.

When the meal was over she left the castle and ran down the steep cliff path to the beach. She stood by the sea's edge and called Hugh's gull: "Keir! Keir!"

He came at once, flying out from the Black Rock. Maisie took him in her hands and remembered what Hugh had told her long ago. She searched in her heart for words that would make a spell:

"Fly to my brother by land and sea
Tell him the queen means harm to me."

Then she tossed the gull up into the air and saw him turn inland, towards the west. She watched him until her eyes hurt – and when she looked down again Inga was standing beside her.

"You will not escape," the queen said.

Chapter Four

The Messenger

For two years Hugh lived with Thomas, and learned the woodcutter's trade. Thomas cut the boy's hair, and gave him clothes like those he wore himself. Hugh washed his fine prince's clothes and laid them away in a chest, under the winter blankets.

"You'll be safe here," Thomas said. "There are no neighbours to go poking their noses in, and when we go to town I'll say you're my cousin's lad, come to work for me."

And Hugh *did* work. Soon his hands were calloused and his skin brown, and the fine clothes were too small even if he had wanted to wear

them. Thomas treated him like the son he had
never had, and Hugh worked all day in the forest
and was happy.

But he never forgot Maisie.

On the day that Keir flew into the clearing
Hugh was chopping wood. The smaller branches
had to be cut from the felled trunks and stacked
and tied ready to be taken to town on market day,
and there was plenty to be done before sundown.
Across the clearing Thomas was hard at work.

The sun slanted low between the tree trunks, and Hugh squinted as he saw the bird fly towards him. At first he didn't see that it was a gull. Then it settled on his shoulder and tweaked his hair with its beak – and he knew. This was his own gull sent by Maisie to find him. That meant she was in danger.

His heart began to beat fast. He was so far from home. And he must go – at once.

Thomas had heard Hugh's axe fall silent. He left his work and crossed the clearing – slowly, for his joints were stiff.

"What is it?" he asked.

Hugh held the bird in his hands and stroked its feathers. "The time has come," he said.

"Your sister needs you?"

"Yes."

Thomas put a hand on Hugh's shoulder. "Now I shall be lonely. You have been like a son to me."

And Hugh looked at the old man and thought of the companionship of their life in the forest, and he knew he would miss Thomas. But he could not stay.

That evening, Thomas made Hugh a parcel of food for the journey: cold meat, and bread and herbs, and a leather bottle full of water. And he told him, "You must take Trusty."

Hugh was shocked. Trusty was Thomas's only horse. He was old, like his master, but he did well enough taking the wood to market. He lived in the stable next to the house and Hugh knew that Thomas loved him. "You can't give me Trusty," he said.

"I have the gold that Randal gave me," said Thomas. "Enough to buy another horse. Trusty is old and slow but he's the best gift I can offer you."

They went across to the stable, and Thomas stroked the horse's bony head.

"I'll tell you something about Trusty," he said. "I was given him by a fairy. Aye, it's true! You needn't look so doubtful. There's fairies come in all shapes and kinds, and this one – a little thin-faced, red-headed thing, she was – she was down on her luck: lost, and hungry; so I gave her food and set her on her way, and she left me the horse as a gift. He didn't look much of a horse, even then, but she says to me, 'He'll do what he's needed to do, and one day he'll do more.' That's what she said: 'One day he'll do more.' And I reckon that time has come."

"What did she mean?" asked Hugh.

"Who knows? These fairies always speak in riddles."

"But won't she be angry if you give away her gift?"

"The horse is mine to give," said Thomas. "And maybe the fairy will watch over you if you ride him. I reckon she's never far away from him, though I've not seen her again."

In the morning Hugh found Keir perched on the windowsill outside the door.

"You must go back to Maisie," he said. And he took the gull in his hands and made a spell:

"Fly to my sister by land and sea
Tell her I come to set her free."

Then he tossed the bird up into the air and watched it fly away between the trees, north-eastwards.

North-eastwards: through the trackless forest, across moor and marsh and mountain.

How will I ever find the way, he wondered?

Chapter Five

Magic on the Moor

In all the time he had lived with Thomas, Hugh had never strayed far into the forest. He didn't know its extent, and could not remember the way he had come with Randal.

"The sun will guide you," said Thomas. And when Hugh set off, riding on Trusty, the dawn was on his right. But as the day went on clouds covered the sun, and soon the sky was grey and the forest dark and shadowy; the paths disappeared and Hugh feared they were travelling in circles.

For a long time there was no sound but the twitter of birds and the crack of twigs under

Trusty's hooves. Then Hugh heard a rustling in the undergrowth. He tensed, fearing wild boar.

But it was not a boar. It was a fox: a red fox with a bushy tail who stood and stared at him with bright eyes, then trotted away amongst the trees. Or *was* it a fox? For just before it slipped out of sight, Hugh thought he caught a glimpse of a woman with red-brown hair, and a sharp pale face that glanced back at him. He remembered the red-haired fairy that Thomas had met; he remembered, too, the fox who had led him and Randal to Thomas's door.

I must follow her, he thought. And he urged Trusty forward.

The forest was dense and dark, but he saw a flicker of red in the undergrowth and went after it. For hours it led him on a winding trail. If he looked at the creature he saw only a fox. But if he half-glanced away he sometimes saw, out of the corner of his eye, the slight figure of the fairy moving ahead, and knew that she was leading him out of the forest.

At last he came upon a glade, where pools of sunlight lay between the trees. He rode through it, on to a widening path, and saw light ahead where the trees ended.

The fox slipped away, back into the forest. It had brought Hugh to the next stage of his journey. Ahead of him lay the open moor.

For two days he rode north-eastwards across the moor, guided by the sun. The food Thomas had given him was almost gone. Trusty was tired and plodded slowly, and Hugh began to long for a horse fit for a prince, one that would take him

swiftly to his castle, to find out what danger Maisie was in. But each day he gave time to the old horse. He let him rest, and patted him, and rubbed him down, and led him to a stream to drink.

On the third day, towards evening, they turned a corner and came upon an old woman sitting beside the path with a bundle of firewood beside her. She looked weary, as if she had carried the wood a long way.

Hugh didn't want to stop. He was desperate to go on, to find Maisie. But he said, "Can I help you, mother?"

The old woman stood up and seized the bridle with a surprisingly strong hand. "I am hungry, lad. Do you have food?"

"I have only a small piece of bread," said Hugh, "but you are welcome to share it."

And he broke the last of his bread in two and gave the larger portion to the old woman.

She ate it quickly and asked, "Do you have water, lad?"

Hugh gave her the leather water bottle that he had refilled at a stream. She drained it all.

Hugh wanted to leave her now and ride on. But it seemed churlish. He asked, "Which way is your home, mother? Can I carry your bundle?"

"You can," said the old woman. She pointed – not north-eastwards, as he had hoped – but to a path that led west across the moor. "And you can let me ride," she added, "and rest my bones."

Hugh had never felt so unwilling, but he helped her up on to Trusty's back, and took the bundle of firewood on to his own back.

"Lead the horse," the old woman said, "but slowly, slowly. Don't jolt my bones."

And so they set off, Hugh leading Trusty at a pace so slow it was scarcely bearable; and all he wanted to do was ride, and ride, as fast as he could, and rescue Maisie from whatever was threatening her.

The path stretched on, and there was no cottage in sight.

It was almost dark when at last they came to a little house, low and green, and roofed with turf; and the old woman said, "Here is my home."

Hugh put down the bundle, then turned to help her dismount; as he did so she seemed to straighten and grow taller, and for a moment he thought he glimpsed a young, sharp face, and a lock of red-brown hair escaping from her hood; and then it was gone, and he saw the old woman again.

"You have been kind to me," she said, "and I shall give you a gift in return."

She brought from the folds of her cloak a ring. It was old and worn, with no pattern on it, and Hugh thought it was too big, but when he put it on it seemed to mould itself to fit his finger. The old woman said, "If you turn the ring on your finger three times sunwise it will turn your enemy's spell back upon its sender. One day, soon, you will need this power."

Hugh stared at the ring. And when he looked up, the old woman was gone, and her house with her, and he and Trusty were alone on the moor, with no food or water, and night coming on.

So the old woman was the fox fairy, thought Hugh. And she has given me a ring of power. But what use is this ring to me now? We are more tired, more hungry, and more lost than ever. Nothing has changed.

But he was wrong. Trusty had changed.

Chapter Six

The Fairy Horse

Trusty shook his head, and Hugh looked up, startled, at the sound of jingling.

He could not believe what he saw. When he left home the horse's bridle had been plain, well-worn leather. Now it was embossed with patterns and hung with silver bells. There was a saddle that smelt of new leather; it was richly decorated in red and silver, and from it hung a water bottle and bulging saddlebags.

"Trusty . . . ?" said Hugh.

But was it Trusty? The horse Hugh saw before him was sleek and young; his mane felt silky, his legs were long, his eyes deep and bright.

And yet they were Trusty's eyes. Hugh looked into them and knew the old horse at once, and Trusty snorted and nuzzled his shoulder in the way that Hugh remembered.

It was Trusty indeed, but in his true form – given back his youth and power.

Hugh saw a name on the bridle, set in gold: *Falomar*. Was this Trusty's real name? His fairy name? For now Hugh had no doubt that this was a fairy horse.

"But I'll always think of you as Trusty," he said, and he stroked the horse's soft nose.

There was hay in the saddlebags and, for Hugh, meat and a new loaf – fresh and warm. When they had eaten, Hugh led Falomar to a stream where they both drank.

"We'll rest till morning," he said.

But Falomar pawed the ground, trembling and eager; he shook his head and the bridle bells rang.

He wants to go now, thought Hugh.

He mounted the fairy horse as the moon was rising. At once, with a great leap, Falomar was away.

They rode like the wind, so fast, so high, that Hugh felt as if stars were streaming through his hair. They plunged into the valley and clattered through sleeping towns where Falomar's hooves struck sparks from the cobbles; they galloped through deep woods padded with pine needles; found fairy paths that only Falomar could see; they leapt rivers like salmon and swam through moon-silvered lakes. And at dawn they reached the coast and saw the gleam of morning on the sea.

On its cliff above the sea stood the castle, with flags flying from its turrets. But all around was devastation: fields of bent and broken crops; a barn with one wall destroyed and the roof caved in; and a trail of crushed grass as wide as a road that led across the field, over the cliff, and into the sea.

Hugh heard sobbing, and saw a woman gathering a few stalks of barley that had escaped whatever destroyed the fields.

"What has happened?" he asked.

The woman wiped her eyes with a dirty hand. "It's the serpent." She stared at Hugh. "You must be a stranger here?"

Hugh hesitated before saying, "Yes."

"Every night it comes," the woman said, "roaming around the headland, trampling the crops. Anything in its way is knocked down. And it howls like a lost soul – enough to wake the dead."

"What does it want?"

"We don't know. It circles the castle and tries to scale the walls; sometimes it beats its head against the gates, but they are too strong. And always, at dawn, it goes: back to its cave under the Black Rock."

"The Black Rock?"

The cave under the Black Rock was Hugh's old hiding-place: his and Maisie's.

"Maisie . . ." he began.

"Maisie?" the woman said. "The Lady Maisie? She's gone. They say the serpent took her."

Chapter Seven

The Serpent

My sister is dead, thought Hugh. And he began to tremble. It couldn't be true. He ran to the clifftop and saw a dark shape submerge near the Black Rock. Its wake still lay on the sea.

The serpent. He imagined it coiled in Maisie's cave, and the image filled him with horror. Had the creature killed his sister?

He heard the seagulls crying as they circled above the cliff.

"Keir!" he called.
"Are you there? Keir!"

At once a gull
detached itself from

47

the flock and flew down to him, alighting on his shoulder. He felt its familiar weight, the scrape of its claws, and saw its flight feathers lifting in the breeze.

"Keir," he said. He stroked the bird's feathers, taking comfort from it.

When he looked back he saw that the woman was still there, in the field, watching him.

"You're not a stranger, are you?" she said, as he approached. There was hope in her voice. "You knew the name of the king's daughter. And the gull knows you."

Hugh felt he could trust her. "I am the prince," he said. "Hugh."

She dropped to her knees. "It's what we longed for! Sir, the kingdom is in trouble. The queen has bound your father with her spells. He's like a shadow. She has all the power and she is a cruel ruler. Even her servant, Randal, is afraid of her, though he is a good man and tries to protect us. We have been praying for your return."

"And I *will* help you!" Hugh promised eagerly.

The people believed in him; he couldn't fail them now. He would challenge Inga and save his father and his kingdom.

But first he must find out what had happened to Maisie.

"What *is* the serpent?" he asked the woman. "Where has it come from?"

She shook her head. "Randal is close to the queen. He might know more."

Yes, thought Hugh, I need Randal.

The gull shifted on his shoulder; its feathers brushed his cheek.

"Keir! You shall be my messenger," said Hugh.

He took the bird in his hands and made a spell:

"Fly to the castle, past gate and key
Tell my friend Randal to come to me."

Then he tossed it up, and Keir flew away, riding on the wind, fast, towards the battlements.

Hugh turned to the woman. "The queen must not know that you have met me. No one must know."

"I won't tell," she promised.

When she had gone Hugh mounted Falomar again. But instead of riding boldly towards the castle with its fluttering pennants, he turned inland, and circled round his home, till he reached the clifftop on the far side. A path led down the cliff to a small cove. He thought Falomar would never manage the steep path, but the fairy horse stepped light as a bird and brought him safely to the beach.

Hugh dismounted. He went to a cleft in the cliff-face. There, where he and Maisie used to hide it, safe from Inga, was their sailing boat.

He looked it over. The boat was sound. Maisie had been taking care of it.

He thought of Maisie, left behind with Inga, waiting. She had sent for him – but was he too late?

He stared across the glittering water.

He was afraid. So much trust had been put in him. By Maisie – who sent the gull. By the woman. By the people who had longed for his return. The weight of it all was heavy; he felt lonely and tired. He fed Falomar, and left the horse guarding the entrance to the cleft while he went inside. Then he lay down in the boat and fell asleep.

When he woke it was dusk. The beach lay in the shadow of the cliff and the gleam had gone from the sea.

Something had disturbed him. He sat up. There was a fluttering at the entrance to the cleft, and Keir flew down and perched on Falomar's saddle. And then Hugh heard the crunch of shoes on pebbles, and a whisper: "My lord? Hugh?"

"Randal!" With a sob Hugh ran to him. They threw their arms around each other. Hugh tried not to cry, but it was impossible now that he was no longer alone.

Randal stood back and held Hugh at arm's length. "You've grown. You have become a true prince."

Hugh told him all about his journey, and the fairy woman, and Falomar; and Randal admired the fairy horse and heard with wonder how he had brought Hugh home. He told Hugh that the queen grew more cruel as her power increased. "But the people believe in you," he said. "They believe you can overcome her enchantment."

"And will you help me?" Hugh asked.

"All I can." He sighed. "I have no power, Hugh. I failed to save Maisie. She has gone. No one saw what happened."

"Was it Inga? Is the serpent her creature?"

"I think so. I think she created it to destroy your sister. Lady Maisie grew strong and beautiful and she defied the queen. Inga hated her. But the serpent has a power of its own. She can't control it now."

"And Maisie?" said Hugh. "Is she—"

But Randal stopped him. "Look!" he said. "It's coming!"

Out by the Black Rock Hugh saw a disturbance in the sea: the waves splashed briefly higher around the entrance to the cave. Then the water settled, but under the surface a long dark shape was moving towards them.

Chapter Eight

Where is Maisie?

"Hide!" said Randal.

They squeezed into the cleft. Hugh pulled Falomar in after him, and saw how the fairy horse seemed to shrink and fade, his brightness dimmed. Keir alighted on a ledge and folded his wings.

They heard the creature before they saw it: a long, wailing howl that seemed to echo from the depths of the sea. Enormous sadness was carried in the sound. Then Hugh heard the scrape of the scaly body dragging itself up the beach, and suddenly, close by, another howl. He looked out and saw a huge lizard-like head, streaming sea water, turning from side to side, questing.

It knows we are near; perhaps it smells us, he thought. And he wanted to melt back into the rock wall. He was afraid – and yet, even though the creature had taken Maisie, its sad cry made him feel pity.

The scraping sound came again. He heard the rattle of claws on pebbles. Peering between his fingers he saw the length of the creature flowing past and upwards, coil on coil, and realised it was scaling the cliff. He knew its claws would be at the top while its tail still slapped the beach.

"It goes towards the castle," whispered Randal. "Each night it climbs the cliff and makes its way there, trampling whatever lies in its path. The people will be out now, ready to try and drive it away. But it won't leave the headland till morning."

"And – Maisie?" said Hugh. "What happened to her? Is my sister dead?"

"No one saw it take her," said Randal. "But I can't give you much hope. She has not been seen since the serpent first appeared."

Hugh thought about this. He didn't want to believe his sister was dead – that the fox fairy and Falomar and Keir had brought him here for nothing. He stepped out of the cleft and stared across the water at the Black Rock. "She might be in the cave," he said. "A prisoner."

Randal came and stood beside him. "All this time? What would she live on?"

"The gulls would feed her. And the seals. They'd all care for her." He made a decision. "I must leave Falomar hidden here and go to the cave. Tonight – while the serpent is away."

Randal shook his head. "Listen, my lord: the queen grows daily more powerful and dangerous. She stands at the window in her tower and watches the sea. If she sees us—"

"Not us," said Hugh. "I shall go alone."

"I can't leave you!"

"You must." Hugh felt sure that it was he alone who should challenge Inga's power. "Go back," he said, "before she misses you. Only – be ready to help me, to let me in, when I come to the castle. And I *will* come, Randal, and bring Maisie with me."

Randal seemed to recognise the new authority in Hugh's voice. He put a hand on the boy's shoulder. "I'll be ready. Now let me help you launch the boat."

Between them they carried the boat down the beach. Keir flew out from the cleft and perched on Hugh's shoulder. Hugh glanced up at the clifftop. There was no sign of the serpent, but he heard a distant sound of voices raised in alarm; blazing torches were moving to and fro.

He climbed into the boat. "Go now!" he whispered. "And wait for me!"

"Good luck be with you," said Randal.

Hugh raised the sail; and as the wind filled it he began to take the familiar route out to the Black Rock. A full moon shone, helping him steer safely, and the sea was calm; and yet he felt afraid – more than he'd admitted to Randal. The serpent was away, but what else might he find?

On the rock the gulls shifted and murmured. They were restless, as if they sensed danger.

Now the mouth of the cave lay open ahead of him. He heard the slap of waves on stone, all the little sounds of the sea: sucking, grinding, hissing, and a deep boom of surf far back in the cave. But no human sound; no sound of Maisie.

Hugh steered the boat closer. He took a breath. "Maisie?" he called softly.

Nothing – but the gulls roosting on the rock cried out a warning.

And then came another sound: a rushing sound overhead. He looked up, and saw a black mass approaching, filling the sky. Birds!

Keir flew up in alarm and Hugh screamed as dark beating wings descended on the boat: birds with hooked claws oustretched, ready to tear; screeching, shrilling, flapping.

They knocked Hugh's hands from the tiller; he crouched to protect himself from their beaks and claws. They settled on the mast, on the sail – which they shredded – on the planks, on his shoulders, on his head and back. He lost control of the boat and it began drifting away from the cave, out to sea.

I must fight back, thought Hugh. He felt desperate. He had failed. Failed at the first move. The queen had been watching from her tower all the time. And now even Keir had left him.

Chapter Nine

Inga's Spells

Hugh struggled to fight off Inga's birds, but as fast as he drove one away another flew at him out of the darkness with fierce cries. The sail had huge rents in it. He tried to bring the boat around while he beat at the creatures with his bare hands, but it was of no use: he was still drifting out to sea.

From overhead came another rush of wings. More are coming, he thought, and he began to despair. But something was different. The clamour in the air above increased. He realised that the birds were no longer attacking him; they were under attack themselves – from gulls!

The gulls of Black Rock were driving away Inga's birds. In the dark of night the whole colony had risen as one and turned on the enemy.

Inga's birds fought back, but they were no match for the great tide of gulls flying out from Black Rock. The dark-winged birds began to scatter.

Soon only the voices of gulls could be heard. As the sky lightened Hugh saw the last of Inga's birds flying in a dark defeated knot towards the shore. The gulls circled protectively above the boat.

Hugh had survived. But he could not stop trembling. There was blood on his hands and face and the wounds were beginning to hurt.

I wish Randal was here, he thought.

Keir dropped down and settled on his shoulder. Hugh stroked him. The bird made him feel braver.

I must steer for the cave, he decided. I don't have much time.

He had been swept far out to sea. The shore was a distant line, darker than the dark sky, and the Black Rock was visible only because waves broke in white foam around it.

He steered for the rock, and the tattered sail took the wind. The boat drew steadily closer, the gulls above it like a shield; and slowly the sky lightened.

He was almost at the cave when he glanced towards the beach and saw the serpent sliding into the sea.

The serpent swam underwater, out of Hugh's sight. But the little boat was close – almost there. I have time, Hugh thought; and his heart beat fast. I still have time. I'll get there first: go into the cave, find Maisie, fetch her out—

But the serpent had reached the Black Rock. It raised its great head from the water, and Hugh knew that it had seen him.

Chapter Ten

The Serpent Strikes

The serpent plunged, humping its scaly back. It rose up under the boat and Hugh felt himself being lifted and hurled towards the rocks.

He clung to the tiller.

He heard the crack of wood splintering on stone. Desperately he tried to push the boat out of danger, but the serpent returned, and banged it back on to the rocks again. A hole appeared in the bow: water rushed in.

It'll sink! thought Hugh.

He leapt out, threw himself onto the rocks and clung there, drenched by crashing waves. Above him he saw flights of gulls swoop down on the serpent like arrows – but the huge creature shook them off, and they circled away, filling the air with their cries.

Hugh struggled higher. The rocks were wet and slippery with weed and the sea smacked into him with a force that knocked the breath from his body. He reached a ledge above the height of the waves and clung there, exhausted.

Looking back, he saw the serpent buffeting the little boat, banging it over and over against the rocks. He saw planks splinter, the mast break in half and fall, the sails go down.

At last nothing remained but broken pieces of wood floating on the sea. The serpent began to move away, towards the cave. Hugh felt relief.

I'm safe, he thought – for the moment, at least.

But he was wrong.

As the serpent turned around, its coils unwound like the coils of a spring, and the tip of its huge tail slapped the rocks and swept him into the sea.

The Serpent Strikes

Hugh went down and down. But he was a strong swimmer. He fought his way to the surface and rose, gulping air.

Across rolling waves he saw the wreckage of the boat floating all around. In front of him was the Black Rock and the open mouth of the cave. He knew that inside the cave was the serpent. But was Maisie there?

Chapter Eleven

Into the Cave

Now, thought Hugh, I must challenge the serpent. He knew that unless he could face Inga's creature, and rescue Maisie, he could not hope to defeat the queen herself.

The only weapon he had was a small knife, useless against that thick scaly hide. He had no chance – and yet there were forces on his side: the fox fairy, the gulls, perhaps the cave itself. He had hope.

"Serpent!" he shouted. And his voice boomed and echoed under the arch of the cave-mouth. "Come out and fight!"

There was a rushing sound, and he realised it was the serpent's breath reverberating in the depths of the cave; and then he heard the scrape of its claws on stone, and a wave rolled out of the cave and struck him, stinging his eyes with spray. And when he was able to see again the creature was there, its huge head reaching almost to the roof.

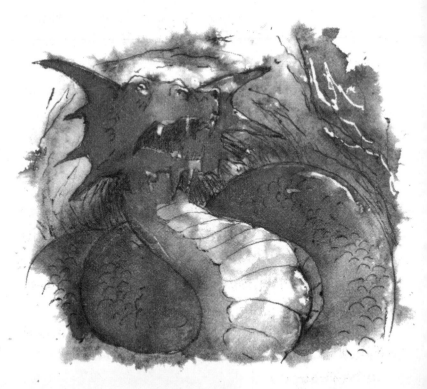

Hugh recoiled in fear. The serpent was enormous. And he didn't know what its powers were – only that Inga had created it. He fought back the instinct to dive and swim away. He had to find Maisie.

"Where is my sister?" he demanded.

He braced himself, expecting the creature to attack him, as it had attacked the boat. But it didn't. Its manner changed. It turned its head away. And then it began to move back into the cave.

Hugh was bewildered. Was it going to *fetch* Maisie?

"Maisie!" he shouted. "Are you there?"

But all he heard was the slap of water on the rocks and the sound of the serpent retreating into the cave.

Hugh was afraid. It was worse than seeing the serpent, not knowing what it was doing. Perhaps this was a trap. Perhaps the creature hoped to lure him into the cave and make him a prisoner, along with Maisie.

He tried once more: "Serpent! Are you afraid of me? Come out and fight!"

Nothing.

Hugh made a decision. He took a deep breath, and swam into the cave.

The rock shelved gently upwards, and soon he was able to get to his feet and wade until he reached the dry area at the back. Here, a passage twisted to the left.

Hugh knew the cave well. He knew how the passage widened and then opened up into a great chamber above the level of the sea. He followed the familiar route, moving cautiously, trying to make no sound as he reached the chamber.

Ahead of him, in the gloom, he could see the green glistening scales of the coiled serpent.

He waited, letting his eyes become accustomed to the half dark. Soon he could see more: the serpent's head, turned away from him, the familiar walls and ceiling of the cave. But not Maisie. Only the great ugly creature filling all the space that had once been theirs.

The serpent has killed her, he thought.

He drew his knife.

The creature heard it. The huge head swung round and down till it was level with his own.

Instinctively Hugh backed away from the half open jaws. But the serpent did not attack. Its eyes stared into his: great dark eyes, full of sorrow.

And Hugh recognised the eyes, and understood.

"Maisie!" he cried.

Chapter Twelve

The Broken Spell

The knife fell with a clatter to the rock. Hugh threw his arms around the serpent's neck and kissed its scaly face.

At once everything changed. The serpent disappeared, revealing the cave in all its echoing spaciousness. And at the centre of that space stood a girl – taller than he remembered – with long brown hair and dark eyes.

"Maisie," said Hugh. "Oh, Maisie!" He ran and hugged her.

"You're hurt!" she said. "Hugh, you're bleeding!"

"It doesn't matter."

Both were crying, but they were tears of happiness.

"I couldn't fight you," said Maisie. "When I saw the boat I thought it was men from the headland coming to taunt me; they often come. So I attacked. But then I heard your voice …"

"Did Inga do this to you?" demanded Hugh.

"Yes. She said, 'No one will ever call you bonny again.' She struck me with a little silver wand; and I felt myself changing – growing huge, scaly, monstrous … I begged her to free me; I begged the guards to let me into the castle, but my voice was not my own, and they shut the gates on me. All they saw was an ugly serpent. Everyone was afraid of me, and I was ashamed of my ugliness. So I came here, to our cave. But, Hugh, the gulls didn't know me! And the seals don't bask here any more. Everything was afraid of me. I would swim out at night and call to Father and try to find a way in to the castle, but the people drove me away."

"They'll know you now," said Hugh. "We'll go back, and together we'll challenge Inga and free our father."

But Maisie turned to him in alarm. "Hugh, you don't understand how powerful Inga is. If we go back to the castle she will put a spell on us both—"

"Don't be afraid," said Hugh – though *he* was afraid. And yet, he thought, I have Falomar, and the magic ring; surely the fox fairy's gifts will not fail me?

He led the way out of the cave, and they swam past the wreckage of the little boat and back to the shore. As they walked up the beach Keir flew out from the Black Rock and landed on Maisie's shoulder and nibbled her hair.

Maisie was overjoyed. "He knows me again!" she said.

Then they heard a soft whinny from the cleft where Hugh had left Falomar. Hugh told Maisie about the fairy horse and the ring.

Falomar regained his brightness as he stepped out of the shade. Maisie exclaimed in delight. "Oh! He's beautiful!" She stroked his nose and mane and admired the silver bells on his harness.

Hugh, streaming sea water from his clothes and hair, mounted the horse. Maisie climbed up behind him, and together they rode to the castle with Keir flying above them.

The fairy horse galloped so fast his hooves barely skimmed the ground. He galloped up to the castle gates – and the astonished guards, on Randal's order, flung them open and let him through. A murmur of amazement ran through the crowd of soldiers and servants: "The children are here! Hugh and Maisie! The children have come back!"

The news grew and spread like a ripple on water. Doors were opened; people ran out to stare. High above the courtyard windows were flung wide; soldiers watched from the battlements as Falomar clattered across the stone courtyard and Hugh, leaping down, beat on the doors of the great hall.

They opened – for no one could withstand Hugh now. And no one wanted to. He had come home, bringing their lost princess, and now he would save the king from Inga's magic.

Falomar scarcely paused. Hugh sprang back into the saddle. They rode straight into the hall where the king sat with Inga. Falomar's hooves clanged on stone, then thudded on the soft snake-patterned carpet that led to the thrones. The servants scattered.

The king stared, bewildered, unable to believe what he saw. "Hugh?" he murmured, struggling to his feet. "Hugh? Maisie?"

Inga had been playing the bone harp. She laid it aside and stood up. She was tall – tall and terrifying – and her glimmering beauty had hardened to the gleam of ice. She hissed with a sound like a sword being drawn.

"You!" she said.

Hugh dismounted, and Maisie sprang down and stood beside him. In the open doorway of the hall the people crowded.

Hugh seized the bone harp and broke it in half and flung it down.

"You have bewitched the king," he said, "but your enchantment will not work on us. We have come to set him free—"

Inga laughed. "You are too late! Look at him: he is mine. The castle is mine, and every creature in it—"

From above her came Keir, swooping and diving around her head, drowning her words with his harsh cry.

Inga put up her hands as if to protect herself. But then she stretched them out towards the gull and began to sing a little strange tune that made Hugh think of snakes with flickering tongues. He saw Keir wobble in mid-flight, turn unsteadily, then slowly flutter to the ground, where he fell on to his side and lay unmoving.

"Keir!" Maisie ran to the bird. She took his limp body in her hands, and tried to breathe life back into him.

Hugh felt a surge of grief that blazed into anger. He turned on the queen. "None of this is yours! You have no place here. Leave now—"

"Leave!" Inga's scorn rang out. "Do you think I am afraid of children?" From nowhere, it seemed, she produced a narrow silver wand. She pointed it at Hugh's heart.

"Hugh!" screamed Maisie. "The ring!"

Hugh touched the ring on his finger. He felt a force rushing towards him, threatening to swallow him up, and he struggled to concentrate, to turn the ring: once … twice … three times sunwise. The force surged around him, and then, abruptly, it was gone. He was free.

But Inga staggered. She shrieked, and dropped the wand.

And then she began to shrink. She grew smaller and smaller, her features bloating, her voice deepening to a croak. Her skin turned dark and blotchy, her eyes bulged, her arms and legs shortened –

"A toad!" cried Maisie.

Inga was gone. But a large brown toad crouched on the floor. Hugh moved towards it, and it hopped. He moved again, forcing it to hop in front of him. He drove it down the length of the hall, and the people parted to let it out of the door. They watched as it hopped across the courtyard, through the gateway, down into the ditch, and out of sight.

Chapter Thirteen

Celebration

He had won.

Hugh was trembling so much he thought he would fall. His father ran and caught him in his arms. The king looked stronger already and the colour had come back to his face. "I should have protected you," he said. "But I have been away – I don't know where."

Hugh clung to him. "It was Inga's magic."

"But it's gone now," said Maisie. "Look!"

Keir was fluttering between her hands. She opened them, and he flew up and settled on the back of the king's throne, bright and bold as ever.

Maisie ran to her father and brother.

"Everything has changed," she said.

Hugh looked around. The bone harp, the snake-patterned carpet and the hangings with their twining patterns had vanished. Where the silver wand had lain was a heap of dust. The dogs had come back into the hall; they thrust their wet noses under the children's hands. A hubbub of voices rose. Randal broke through the crowd and knelt to the king and promised to stay and serve him.

Then Hugh saw that Falomar had changed too. Gone were his bridle bells, his red and silver harness. Gone, too, was his youth. He was just an old, tired horse once more.

"Trusty!" said Hugh. He went to the horse and patted him and stroked his nose. Trusty neighed softly – and for a moment, as he tossed his mane, Hugh caught a faint sound of bells and saw a sparkle in the air around him; and he knew that if ever he was needed again Trusty was still a fairy horse.

The king turned to the people. He clapped his hands and called for silence.

"We must have a feast!" he said, "for the three of us, who have all returned from enchantment."

And the people cheered.

A week of preparation began: the cooks created a wondrous cake, the musicians practised new songs, and the dressmakers measured Maisie and Hugh, exclaimed at how they'd grown, and began cutting cloth.

The people from the villages around were invited, and lords and ladies from all over the kingdom. And Hugh sent Keir with a special invitation – though I don't know if she'll come, he thought.

On the night of the feast, flags flew from the battlements, and the musicians played, and there was singing and storytelling and dancing.

Once, changing partners in the dance, Hugh found himself facing a lady with a pale, sharp face and red-brown hair. She took his hand and they stepped and circled twice. Before he could speak, the dance moved them apart, and he didn't see her again; but he had recognised her, and he was smiling as he turned to his next partner.

The celebrations went on all night, and the sounds of laughter and music floated through the open doors and windows. Outside, in the ditch, crouched a large brown toad. "Let me in!" she croaked. "I am the queen! The queen!" But no one heard her.

When dawn came, everyone was asleep. The servants slept in the hall, and Maisie and Hugh and the king slept in their beds with their dogs on the floor beside them.

In his stable Trusty whinnied. He remembered a dream in which he had galloped as fast as the wind.

The sea broke in foam against the Black Rock, where the gulls with their thousand voices were waking. The seals came back to the cave.

Soon Hugh and Maisie would wake and swim out to join them.

h HODDER Another Story Book from Hodder Children's Books

THE FAIRY COW

Ann Turnbull

"You've such a way with the cows, Megan," said Mrs Wynne the washerwoman, "it's a wonder the fairies don't take you to be their dairymaid."

Megan loves to tend her father's cows. And in her free time, she dreams of the lake over the hills. A magical place where magical creatures graze – the fairy cows.

Then Megan's father takes one captive. "She'll make our fortune," he says.

But the fairies are angry, and have their own special way of taking revenge. Only Megan knows the right thing to do . . .

Another Story Book from Hodder Children's Books

IMOGEN AND THE ARK

William Mayne

When Imogen sees the Ark in the toyshop she knows it has to belong to her.

But overnight the shop burns down. Could any toys survive that? The fire engine's hoses cause a flood, but what else is an Ark built for?

How far does the flood reach, what lives in it, what storms rage? Only Imogen sees the terrors of the Ark's journey. Only Imogen sees its long journey home again with its living cargo . . . where she is ready and waiting.

THE LITTLE SEA HORSE

Helen Cresswell

Out of the sea comes an enchanted creature –
a tiny horse of purest white with hooves of
brightest gold.

Molly knows he is far too precious to keep,
but the local townspeople lock the magical
horse in a cage, and throw away the key. Only
Molly can find a way to release him back to
the sea.

A lyrical and deeply evocative tale from a
magical storyteller.

Another Story Book from Hodder Children's Books

THE DRAGON'S CHILD

Jenny Nimmo

"Mother, I'm falling." With a final squeal, the dragon's child slid from his mother's back and fell earthwards through the wind.

Dando the dragon child, abandoned by his mother, must now survive alone, in a place where the dreadful Doggins lurk. Only an orphaned slave girl offers him hope. She knows he is a magical creature, and their special friendship keeps them both safe, for now . . .

An enchanting fantasy from a prize-winning author.

Another Story Book from Hodder Children's Books

MILLY

Pippa Goodhart

It's New Year's Eve. The start of a new
millennium. Alice spends an enchanted
evening with her grandad, while at home
her parents await the birth of a new baby.

It's a magical time, a special moment in history.

But what will it mean for Alice?

h HODDER Another Story Book from Hodder Children's Books

FOG HOUNDS, WIND CAT, SEA MICE

Joan Aiken

Three magical stories from a spellbinding storyteller.

In the first, the Fog Hounds are mysterious – and deadly. They roam the land from dusk to dawn. No one who is chased by them ever lives to tell the tale. But Tad is not afraid. Tad wants one for himself. And when he comes face to face with a Fog Hound puppy, things can never be the same again . . .

The Wind Cat and the Sea Mice have equally strange tales to tell . . .